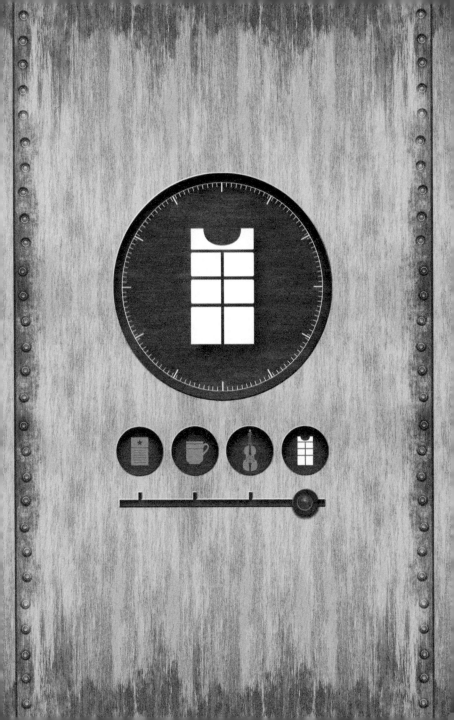

by STEVE BREZENOFF

RETURN TO TITANIC

OVERBOARD

4

ILLUSTRATED by SCOTT MURPHY

STONE ARCH BOOKS · A CAPSTONE IMPRINT

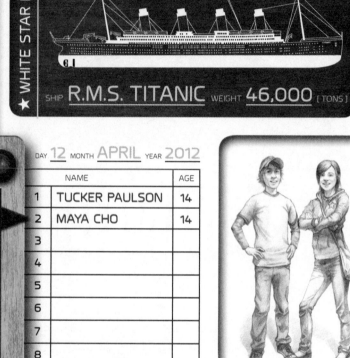

★ WHITE STAR LINE

SHIP **R.M.S. TITANIC** WEIGHT **46,000** [TONS]

DAY 12 MONTH APRIL YEAR 2012

	NAME	AGE
1	TUCKER PAULSON	14
2	MAYA CHO	14
3		
4		
5		
6		
7		
8		

Published by Stone Arch Books - A Capstone Imprint • 1710 Roe Crest Drive, North Mankato, Minnesota 56003
www.capstonepub.com

Library of Congress Cataloging-in-Publication Data is available on the Library of Congress website.
Library binding: 978-1-4342-3302-8 • Paperback: 978-1-4342-3912-9

Summary: Tucker and Maya join the *Titanic* survivors in the lifeboats as they wait and hope for rescue.

Image Credits: Library of Congress: Chronicling America/University of California, Riverside; Riverside, CA, 111; Newscom: Getty Images/AFP/Leon Neal, 110

Editor: Alison Deering
Designer and Art Director: Bob Lentz
Creative Director: Heather Kindseth

Printed in the United States of America in Stevens Point, Wisconsin.
102011 006404WZS12

CONTENTS

NEW YORK

GREENVILLE

★ WHITE STAR LINE
04.12.2012

IN TROUBLE

1

"I'm telling you, it's not here," Maya Cho told her father as she watched him hunt beneath her computer desk for her cell phone.

Maya's father looked up at her from his position below her desk. He pushed aside clothes and crumpled pieces of paper.

"I wish you'd keep your room at least a little cleaner, Maya," he grumbled. "How you find anything in here is beyond me."

"I have a system," Maya said, shrugging. She sat on the edge of her bed and looked at her fingernails. "It works for me."

"Well, then, use your system to find your cell phone," her dad suggested. He stood up, smacking his head on the underside of her desk in the process. "Ow!"

Maya cringed. "Did that hurt?" she said.

"Yes!" he snapped. "You know, if you would help, we'd find your cell phone faster, and maybe I wouldn't have banged my head."

"I *would* help," Maya said, "but I know it's not here. We're just wasting our time."

"Oh, really?" her dad said. "And how can you be so sure with all of this mess?"

"I, um, already looked," Maya said. Truthfully, though, she hadn't looked. She didn't need to. She knew exactly where her phone was — in the bottom of a lifeboat in the middle of the Atlantic Ocean, way back in 1912, where she'd dropped it.

Her father ran his hand over his face in frustration. "If you're so sure it's not here, do you have any idea where it could be?" he asked. "I don't have time to keep searching. I'm going to be late for work."

"It's probably at the museum," Maya said. She stood up and nodded firmly. "Yeah, it must be. I'm almost positive that's the last place I used it."

Her father looked at his watch and sighed. "Fine," he said. "I'll drive you over there. But remember, you are grounded today. You and Tucker are both in serious trouble after what happened at the museum yesterday. If Tucker is there, you won't be hanging out with him."

"I know, I know," Maya said, rolling her eyes. "No fun for Maya today. Got it, Dad."

"We'll go in, get your phone, and leave," her dad said. "Then we're going to my office, where you will sit at the empty desk by the copy machine and do your homework for the rest of the day."

Maya took a deep breath and let it out. "Yes, sir," she said. She gave her father a mock salute. She had every intention of following those orders. But first, she had some time-traveling to do, and she needed to find Tucker in order to carry out her plan.

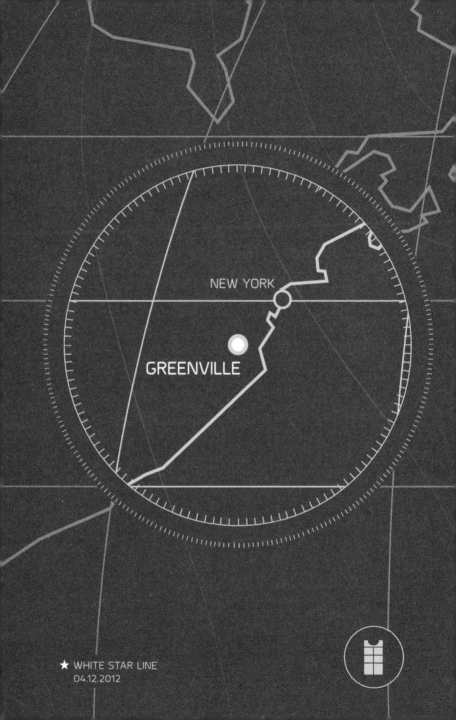

NEW YORK

GREENVILLE

★ WHITE STAR LINE
04.12.2012

THE PLAN

2

"I am so sorry about this, Fiona," Maya's
father said to Mrs. Paulsen, Tucker's mom, as
he and Maya followed her down the hallway at
Greenville History Museum. "Maya insists that
she must have left her phone here."

Maya looked around at the empty hall. The
museum wouldn't open to the public for another
hour, and it was practically deserted. Their
footsteps on the cold marble floor echoed through
the empty building.

"It's no trouble," Mrs. Paulsen said. "I left
Tucker at home today. As long as we're keeping
the kids apart, Maya is welcome here."

Maya rolled her eyes. She was walking a few feet behind the grown-ups, so they didn't see.

"I just don't get what happened yesterday," Mrs. Paulsen said. She came to a stop in front of the meeting room door and flipped through her keys. She had about a hundred of them. "How on earth did Tucker end up soaking wet, anyway?"

She finally found the right key and unlocked the door. She pushed it open, but stopped in the open doorway, lost in thought, for a few seconds.

Maya giggled quietly to herself. "Who knows?" she said. She slid past Mrs. Paulsen and walked into the meeting room.

"Well, I'd think *you* would know," her father said. "You did spend the day with him, didn't you?"

Maya made a show of looking carefully around the meeting room. There weren't many places to look, though, so it didn't take long.

Maya spotted a bowl of hard candies in the middle of the big conference table. She grabbed a few and stuck them in her messenger bag, just

in case. Then she turned around to face her father and Mrs. Paulsen.

"It's not here," Maya said, shrugging. "That's weird. It must be in the storeroom."

She turned to head out the door, but Mrs. Paulsen grabbed her arm and pulled her to a halt.

"Wait a minute," Mrs. Paulsen said. "How could it be in the storeroom? You and Tucker were in here all day yesterday. You weren't supposed to be in the storeroom at all."

"Oh, um . . ." Maya stammered. She frantically tried to come up with a good reason. "I guess I must have lost it two days ago, then."

Mrs. Paulsen and Mr. Cho crossed their arms and stared hard at Maya.

Maya flashed what she hoped was an innocent smile. "That must be it," she said confidently. "I'm sure I haven't seen it since two days ago."

The adults sighed. "Fine," Mrs. Paulsen said. She held up her keys. "Let's go to the storeroom."

Inside the storeroom, Mrs. Paulsen and Mr. Cho stood by the door and watched as Maya looked for her cell phone. She pretended to dig around among the stored exhibits, crates, and packing material strewn about the big room.

Mr. Cho shook his head. "Just think," he said. "Soon they'll be in high school."

Mrs. Paulsen nodded. "Yup," she said. "It's just going to get worse, isn't it?"

Maya took advantage of the adults' distraction. She quickly reached into the Special Collection crate — the collection of magical items from the *Titanic* that had allowed her and Tucker to travel back to 1912 — and grabbed the life vest in its protective wrapper. It was the only item they hadn't used yet and their last chance to save

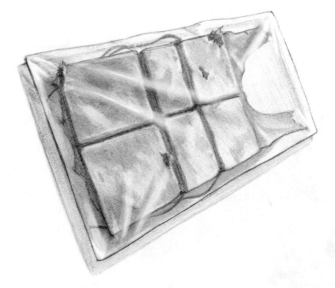

Liam. She slipped it quickly and quietly into her messenger bag.

With the life vest safely stowed away, Maya hopped to her feet. "It's not here, either," she said. She headed back for the door.

"That's it?" her father asked. "This room is enormous, and you've barely even looked. How can you be so sure your phone isn't in here somewhere?"

"Well, it's not like I was all over the room," Maya pointed out. "Tucker and I only worked with the Special Collection. Right, Mrs. Paulsen?"

Tucker's mother nodded in agreement. "It's true," she said. "The kids just worked with that one box. It's why they got in trouble in the first place. If Maya's phone isn't there, it's probably not in the museum."

"Maybe Tucker found it," Maya suggested. "I mean, after I left yesterday."

"I suppose that's possible. . . ." Mrs. Paulsen said, somewhat doubtfully.

Mr. Cho pulled his own cell phone out of his pocket and handed it to his daughter. "Here," he said. "Call him. I'm not wasting a drive over to the Paulsens' house if Tucker doesn't have it. I'm late enough for work as it is."

Maya smiled and took the phone from her father's outstretched hand. She quickly dialed Tucker's number from memory and waited for him to pick up.

"Hi, Tucker," she said cheerfully when he answered. "It's Maya."

"Maya?" Tucker said. He sounded surprised to hear from her. "What's up? I don't think we're supposed to be talking today."

"I'm fine," Maya said. "Listen, did you find my cell phone yesterday?"

"Your phone?" Tucker repeated. "I thought you said you dropped it in the lifeboat or something."

"Oh, great!" Maya said, smiling. She turned to give her dad and Mrs. Paulsen the thumbs-up signal. "And you have it at your house right now?"

"What?" Tucker asked. "Maya, what are you talking about? I don't have your phone. It's probably still in the lifeboat, or at the bottom of the Atlantic, like a hundred years ago."

"Super," Maya said, sounding as upbeat as possible. "My dad's going to drive me over there right now so I can get it. Thanks, Tucker!"

She closed the phone before Tucker could reply and handed it back to her dad. "Okay, let's get over there, Dad," she said. "You don't want to be any later for work, remember?"

NEW YORK

GREENVILLE

★ WHITE STAR LINE
04.12.2012

3

NOW OR NEVER

The second her dad pulled the car to a stop in the Paulsens' driveway, Maya threw her door open and hopped out. "You wait here, Dad," she said. "I'll be right back!" She slammed the car door shut behind her and ran up the brick walkway to Tucker's front door.

"Open up, Tucker," she hollered as she pounded on the door. "It's me."

The door swung open. But Tucker wasn't standing on the other side, as Maya had expected. Instead, a woman who appeared to be in her early twenties stood in the open doorway. Maya had never seen her before.

The woman stood there with her arms crossed and her eyebrows raised. "Well?" she said. "What do you want? Are you selling cookies or something?"

"Um, ha ha," Maya said. "And no. I'm a friend of Tucker's. I have to —"

The girl closed the door halfway. "Tucker is grounded," she said. "He was a naughty boy, and he can't play with his little friends today. Sorry."

Maya forced a smile. She didn't like this babysitter. "I'm not here to 'play,'" she said. Setting her jaw, she pushed through the half-open door.

The babysitter stumbled out of the way. "Hey!" she said. "I said no visitors."

"I'm not visiting," Maya said. She opened the front coat closet on her way past and grabbed a couple of parkas. "I just need to talk to him for a second."

"Why do you need coats?" the babysitter asked.

Maya didn't answer. She just hurried up the stairs.

"Hey!" the babysitter called up the stairs after her. "What's with the coats?"

Maya threw open Tucker's bedroom door and hurried inside. She slammed the door and flipped the deadbolt behind her. "A babysitter?" she said. "What are you, like, five?"

Tucker was so surprised he nearly fell out of his desk chair. "How did you get in here?" he asked.

"I used the front door," Maya said. "Duh. Now put this on. We have work to do." She tossed one of the parkas onto Tucker's bed.

"What are you talking about?" Tucker asked. "And what was with that phone call? You sounded like a crazy person."

Maya ignored him. She dropped her messenger bag on the floor and opened it.

"Seriously, Maya, what's going on?" Tucker asked. "You're acting kind of nuts. It sounded like you were having a totally different conversation on the phone."

Maya looked up at him and rolled her eyes. "I was," she said. "I was talking to the Tucker who isn't a total moron."

"Hey!" Tucker said, looking offended. "What did I do?"

"Nothing," Maya said. She picked up the parka she'd thrown on his bed and held it out to him. "Just put this on."

Tucker took the heavy coat, but he didn't put it on. "Why?" he asked. "First of all, it's April. I don't need a parka. Second, we're not going anywhere. I'm grounded, remember? We both are. Or did you forget about our little adventure yesterday? Me showing up in the meeting room soaking wet didn't exactly go over well with my mom."

Maya rolled her eyes and slipped on the other parka.

"Hey, isn't that my mom's?" Tucker asked.

Suddenly, there was a loud bang on the door. "What's going on in there?" Maya's dad hollered.

"Oh, no," Maya hissed. "Tucker, put on the coat!"

"I told her, no visitors today," the babysitter was saying in the hall. Maya rolled her eyes. That babysitter was really getting on her nerves.

"Maya," her father said. He was starting to sound really angry. "Come out here this instant, young lady!"

"Okay, Dad," Maya called back. "Be right there!" She reached into her messenger bag and pulled out the life vest , still safely enclosed in its plastic bag.

Tucker's eyes went wide. "How did you get that?" he whispered.

"I'll explain later," Maya said quickly. "This is our last chance to save Liam. It's now or never. My dad is about to bust the door down."

As if on cue, Maya's dad banged again. "Maya!" he shouted. "Open this door right now before I break it down!"

"Okay, good point," Tucker said. He pulled on the parka. "Let's go."

Maya nodded and opened the plastic bag. She held the life vest out to Tucker, and together they grabbed hold.

* * *

The next time Maya opened her eyes, she was sitting on a bench in lifeboat sixteen. Turning her head, she saw Tucker lying on the floor of the lifeboat. He was groaning and holding his head like it was pounding.

Maya shivered and pulled the heavy parka tighter around her shoulders. The Atlantic air was freezing, even in April.

"So," she said in a loud voice. Around her, startled lifeboat passengers gasped. "Has anyone seen my phone?"

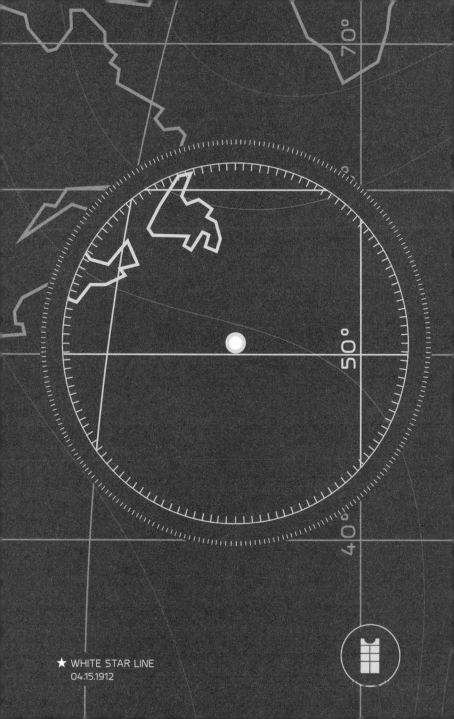

70°

50°

40°

★ WHITE STAR LINE
04.15.1912

4

LIFEBOAT SIXTEEN

"Where did you two come from?" asked Violet Jessop, the *Titanic* stewardess who'd been helping them before they disappeared. "I thought you'd both drowned!" She threw her arms around Maya and Tucker.

"Nope," Maya said, trying to catch her breath as Violet squeezed her tightly. "We're both totally fine."

When Violet finally released them from the hug, she was smiling. Her face glowed red from the cold, but also from relief at finding the two children alive.

Her neighbor in the lifeboat was holding a

baby. It was the one Violet been given charge of not long ago as their lifeboat left *Titanic*. Violet took the infant and held it close.

"I told you we'd be right back," Maya said. She was busy peering around the floor of the lifeboat, trying to locate her cell phone. "We can't really explain any more than that."

"Did you figure out whose baby that is?" Tucker asked, trying to change the subject.

Violet looked down at the infant in her arms. A small smile played on her lips. She shook her head.

"I can't understand it," Violet said. "This baby seems to be entirely on its own. Hopefully I'll find its mum when we get rescued. Maybe she's on one of the other lifeboats."

"I hope so," Maya said, looking down at the infant's sleeping face.

The other passengers of lifeboat sixteen sat quietly, staring at the two kids in awe. Maya and Tucker stood out even more than usual, thanks to the bulky winter parkas they wore. No one seemed to know what to say.

Maya looked from one passenger to the next, waiting for someone to speak up. No one did.

"So," Maya finally said. "My phone. Has anyone seen it?"

"Your phone?" Violet repeated. She wrinkled her forehead in confusion. "What on earth do you mean?"

"My telephone," Maya said. "You people do have telephones, don't you?"

Violet looked at Tucker in confusion, but he just shrugged. *Let Maya try to explain how a cell phone works to people from the twentieth century*, he thought.

"Do you mean the British people?" Violet asked. "Of course we have telephones."

Maya sighed in relief. "Wonderful," she said. "Have you seen mine?"

"Seen it?" Violet said. "How could we have seen your phone?"

"Well, I did drop it on this lifeboat," Maya said. She was beginning to sound exasperated.

"Okay, enough of this," Tucker said finally. He stood up. "Maya," he said, "we have bigger things to worry about than finding your phone."

But Maya wouldn't give up. "My dad is going to kill me if I don't find it," she said, rooting around the bottom of the lifeboat.

"He's not going to kill you," Tucker said. "Just tell him . . ."

"Aha!" Maya exclaimed triumphantly. She sat back up, clutching her cell phone in her fist. "Found it!"

Tucker rolled his eyes. "Great," he said. "Now can we worry about more important stuff?" He looked back at Violet. "How long have you been waiting in the lifeboat?"

"Only a few minutes," she said. "Maya only jumped out a little while ago." That realization seemed to jog her memory. She turned toward Maya, who was busy stowing her phone safely in her bag. "How did you survive that jump?" Violet asked. "And how are you both completely dry?"

"Well . . ." Tucker started to say.

"And where did you get those heavy coats?" Violet went on. "I've never seen anything like them. You two have worn nothing but denim pants and sleeveless cotton shirts this whole trip!"

Tucker and Maya exchanged a quick glance.

"You'd never believe us, even if we told you," Tucker said, shaking his head ruefully. "Ms. Jessop, Have you seen Liam?"

"Liam?" Violet repeated. "You mean that boy from third class you got in trouble with last night?"

Tucker and Maya nodded.

"He's not on this lifeboat, obviously," Violet said. "I haven't seen him since we lost sight of him on the deck." The baby in her arms began to fuss, and she held it more tightly and rocked it a bit.

"Have all the lifeboats launched?" Maya asked.

Violet opened her mouth to reply, but the voices all around drowned her out. The passengers in the lifeboats were shouting and pointing frantically behind Maya and Tucker. They both turned to look.

Behind them was the *Titanic*, its deck tilted steeply and its lights still glowing brightly against the night sky. The massive bronze propellers at the ship's stern were beginning to rise out of the water as the bow plunged beneath the cold, dark surface of the Atlantic Ocean.

Tucker and Maya could hear large items within the ship, probably furniture, crashing toward

the rapidly sinking bow. As the survivors in the lifeboats watched in horror, *Titanic*'s forward smokestack collapsed. The ocean liner's lights flickered once, illuminating the passengers in the water one last time before finally going dark.

Titanic's stern continued to rise until it was almost completely perpendicular to the water. Then, with an deafening crack, the stern of the ship crashed back down against the hard surface of the water. Tucker heard Maya gasp loudly next to him and realized that *Titanic* had literally broken in half.

The broken-off stern section floated level against the water for a few minutes before being pulled vertical again. In moments, the stern section was swallowed up by the cold Atlantic Ocean. The place where *Titanic* had been was filled with passengers splashing in the water. The unsinkable ship was gone.

Maya and Tucker heard quiet crying all around them. In the darkness a voice whispered, "Someone will come. We will be rescued."

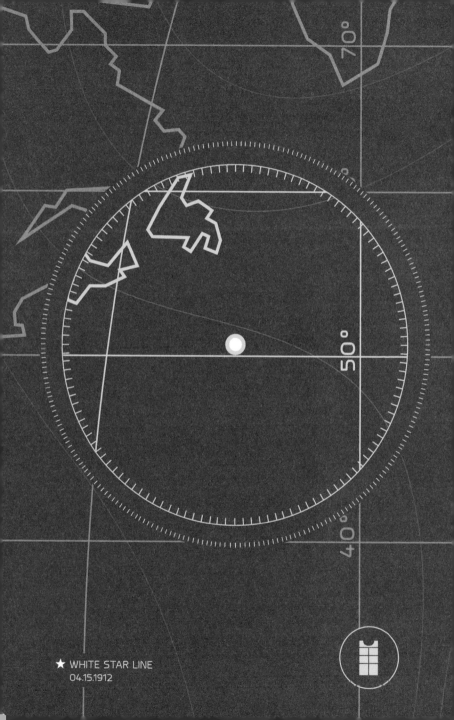

70°

50°

40°

★ WHITE STAR LINE
04.15.1912

5

THE LONG WAIT

Tucker heard the frantic cries and splashing of people struggling against the ocean. Though the water was fairly calm, it was also completely frigid. No one could survive long outside of one of the lifeboats.

"Isn't anyone going to go pick those people up?" Tucker said. "We have to help them!"

Maya leaned anxiously toward the two men working the oars of their lifeboat. "Those people aren't going to survive, treading water like that," she said.

"We can't help them," one of the men said.

"He's right," said the other man. "We can't get too close. The suction of a ship the size of *Titanic* sinking into the ocean is too great. It will pull us down with it."

The first man started rowing, moving the little lifeboat farther away from where *Titanic* had been just moments before. "Besides," he said as he rowed, his voice straining with the effort, "if we try to take this boat into the crowd of people in the water, we'll hurt them or cause utter chaos. We can't have people grabbing onto the sides. They'll capsize us, and we'll all drown!"

"There must be something we can do to help them," Maya insisted.

"I'm afraid not," Violet said quietly. "Trust these men, lass. They are tried and true men of the sea."

The two men on the oars nodded their thanks to Violet. But it didn't make Tucker and Maya feel any better about leaving so many people in the water to fight for their lives on their own.

Just then, one voice became clearer and louder than the rest. It sounded like a child. "Mum!" the voice cried out. "Da! Are you out there?"

"Liam?" Tucker whispered into the darkness.

"It is Liam," Maya said. "He must be looking for his parents."

Tucker spun to face the oarsmen. "Can you find him?" he asked.

One of them shook his head. "Not in this dark, and not without endangering everyone onboard this lifeboat," he said. "But if he is in a boat, he is safe. You'll see him soon."

"But —" Tucker started to plead. He was interrupted by a loud splash nearby.

"Help!" Liam cried.

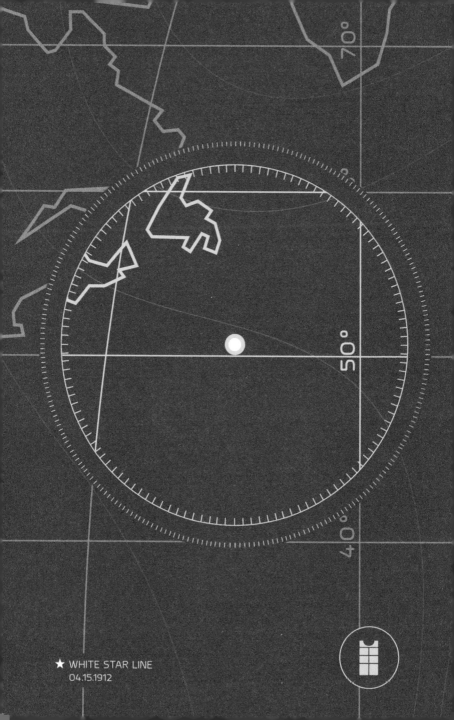

70°

50°

40°

★ WHITE STAR LINE
04.15.1912

MAN OVERBOARD

6

"Please!" Tucker shouted. "We have to help him."

The oarsmen looked at each other. "We can't," one of them said.

"He's just a boy," Violet said. "He's desperate to find his parents. We can't just abandon him."

"Help!" Liam shouted. He splashed and struggled against the cold ocean water. "Help me!" he cried.

"He should stop struggling like that," one of the oarsmen said. "He'll just tire himself more quickly."

"You have to help him!" Maya yelled frantically.

They heard Liam splashing in the water. "He's not far," Tucker said. He leaned over the edge of the lifeboat. "I think I can see him!"

Finally, the oarsmen looked at each other. The oars began to pump and the lifeboat began to glide through the water.

"Thank you both," Violet said gratefully.

Maya and Tucker stayed at the front of the little boat. Soon they could see Liam clearly. He was bobbing up and down. Even with his life vest on, he kept slipping underwater. He was obviously running out of energy — and out of time.

"A little closer!" Tucker shouted to the oarsmen.

Maya leaned over the edge of the lifeboat. "Liam!" she yelled. "We're coming for you!"

She reached out as far as she could and finally felt Liam's wet hand. She grabbed it tightly and tried to pull. "Help me," she said to Tucker.

Tucker leaned out next to her and found

Liam's wrists. Together, they hauled their friend out of the frigid water and into lifeboat sixteen.

Liam lay huddled in the bottom of the little boat, wet and shivering, choking on the saltwater in his throat.

One of the oarsmen found a heavy blanket and passed it to Violet. She quickly leaned down and laid the blanket over Liam's shoulders as he sat up.

"That was a foolish thing you did, lad," the oarsman said. "You could have drowned or frozen to death. You would have, too, if not for these, um, spirited American children."

Liam didn't answer. He didn't even nod or shake his head. He just sat there, shivering.

Maya sat down on the floor of the lifeboat next to him. She put an arm around his shoulders. Quietly, he lowered his head, and though he didn't make a sound, Maya could tell from the way his shoulders shook that he was crying.

Before long, quiet fell over the survivors' stretch of ocean. All the lifeboats had moved away from the sinking ship, and the passengers in the water had stopped splashing. In the silence and the darkness of the night, Tucker leaned closer to Maya. "Have you done any more research?" he whispered.

"About the ship?" Maya whispered back. "About the sinking?"

"Yeah," Tucker said. "Well, more about how the survivors got rescued. Do you know how long we'll be waiting?"

"A couple of hours," Maya said. "Give or take."

Tucker nodded. There was nothing to do but wait.

As the minutes and hours passed, Tucker stared out into the darkness. There was no moon that night. He kept waiting for his eyes to adjust to the darkness, but they never did. He could barely see Violet and Maya on either side of him in the boat. Beyond that, he couldn't see a thing.

Liam had gotten up from the floor of the boat and was sitting on a bench with the other passengers. Maya and Tucker sat on either side of Violet, who still held the baby clutched tightly in her arms.

"If I didn't know any better," Tucker said quietly, "I'd think our little boat was all alone out here."

Maya nodded. Then she said what they'd both been thinking. "I hope Liam's parents are out there someplace," she said.

Glancing over, Tucker saw Violet reach for

Maya's hand and squeeze it reassuringly. He started when realized he could actually see Violet's hand. The night was brightening.

Tucker looked up and found a glimmer glowing on the horizon.

A great blast sounded over the ocean.

"A ship!" someone shouted. "We're saved!"

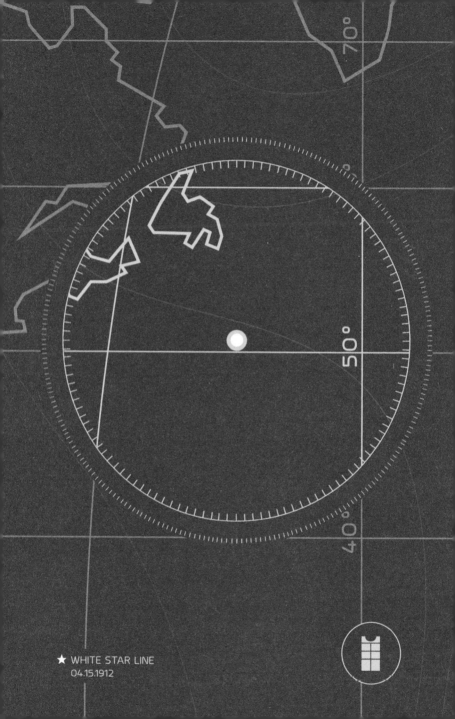

THE
SURVIVORS

7

It took hours to collect all of the survivors in the lifeboats. The ship that arrived, the *RMS Carpathia*, was much shorter and smaller than the *Titanic*. Each lifeboat pulled up alongside the *Carpathia* in turn. The crew of the *Carpathia* hung rope ladders down from the gangway doors, and eventually every survivor climbed into the ship.

"Where is my husband?" Maya overheard a woman asking frantically. "He must be on board. I left him on the *Titanic*!"

Another survivor climbed onto the *Carpathia*,

sobbing. It was impossible to tell if she was crying with relief, or crying over someone who didn't survive. Some survivors cheered for the crew of the *Carpathia*. Others were simply silent, stunned by the amazing events they'd lived through.

By the time all the survivors were onboard, it was after eight in the morning. The sun was up, shining brightly on the survivors now spread out on the *Carpathia*'s deck. Of the 2,223 passengers onboard *Titanic* when it set sail, only 711 had survived.

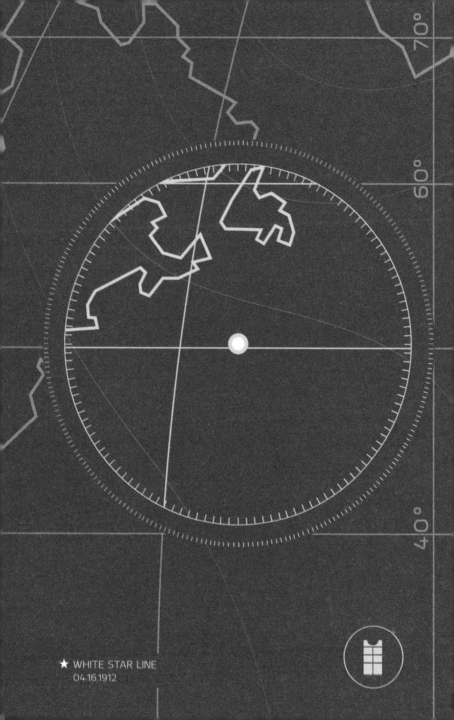

70°

60°

40°

★ WHITE STAR LINE
04.16.1912

A SLIVER OF HOPE

Maya and Tucker walked with Violet on the deck of *Carpathia*. Violet wore a blanket around her shoulders and held the mysterious infant against her chest. Liam had gone off to look for his parents, still clinging to a sliver of hope that they'd found space on a different lifeboat.

As they walked along the deck, Tucker spotted a single figure standing alone near the railing, looking out over the water. At first he couldn't even tell if it was a boy or a girl, because whoever it was was wrapped tightly in a blanket that covered his or her head. But it was definitely

a child — the way the figure was hunched over
made whoever it was appear shorter than Maya
and Tucker.

As Tucker got closer, he started to recognize
the person. He could tell it was Liam just from
the way he stood. His stance was more familiar
than it should have been, having known him for so
short a time. Tucker felt like he'd known this boy
all his life — or longer.

There's something familiar about him, Tucker thought. *I just can't figure out what it is.*

"Liam?" Tucker said quietly. He started to walk faster. Maya jogged to keep up. Tucker hoped against hope that their friend had somehow found his parents.

"Liam?" Tucker called again.

Liam finally raised his head and pulled the blanket down a bit. He turned to look.

Tears streamed down his cheeks. He was alone. He hadn't found his parents. Maya and Tucker reached him.

"Hey!" Violet suddenly shouted from behind them. The three kids turned to look. A woman — completely covered in a blanket — had grabbed the baby. Then she ran off.

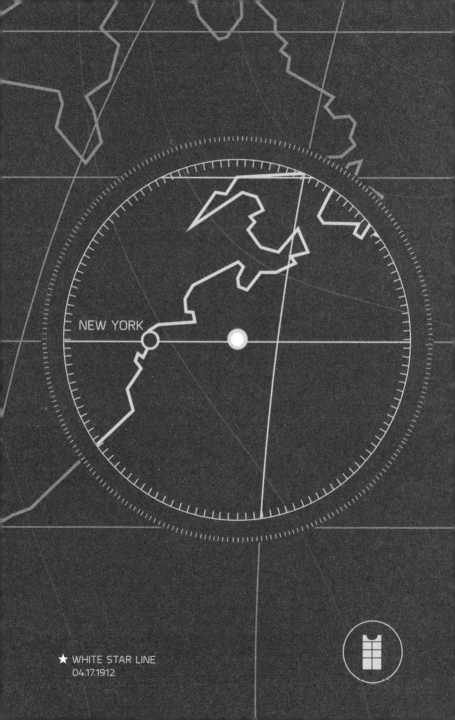

NEW YORK

★ WHITE STAR LINE
04.17.1912

ORPHANS

In the *Carpathia* lounge a few minutes later, Maya kept an arm wrapped tightly around Liam. Tucker could hardly bring himself to look the boy in the face. *I can't even imagine what it would be like to suddenly have no parents*, Tucker thought.

Violet paced back and forth in the small lounge. The *Carpathia* wasn't as luxurious a liner as the *Titanic* had been. This lounge was modest.

"I'm sure it was the poor darling's mother," Violet said, wringing her hands. She was still worrying about the mysterious baby. She glanced at Maya, as if for confirmation. "It was the baby's mother, don't you think?" Violet asked.

Maya smiled and nodded. "I'm sure it was," she said. "The baby is in good hands."

Violet shook her head. "I'm sorry," she said. "I've been worrying about the wrong child." She sat down next to Liam as well.

A *Carpathia* steward came in carrying a chipped mug of tea and held it out to Violet.

"Thank you," Violet said. She took the mug and slipped it into Liam's hands. "Is someone waiting for you in New York, lad?" she asked gently.

Liam nodded. He held the tea in both hands, just under his nose, letting the steam from the hot liquid warm his face. "My aunt," he said.

Violet patted his knee. "Then she will care for you," she said. "I will make sure you find her when we arrive."

"Arrive?" Liam repeated, finally looking up. "Arrive where?"

Tucker realized he hadn't thought about where they'd go next either. The *Titanic* had been headed for America and New York. But the *Carpathia* had started its voyage in New York.

Who knows where we'll end up, Tucker thought.

Violet smiled tightly. She looked at Maya and Tucker, too. "We're leaving any moment," she said. "And we are safe."

A horn sounded. The rumbling of the engines began to rise from the belly of the ship.

The steward stuck his head into the lounge again and said, "Departing for New York City."

NEW YORK

★ WHITE STAR LINE
04.18.1912

10

TO NEW YORK

The journey to New York was a long one. For three days, Tucker, Maya, and Liam slept on cots the *Carpathia*'s crew had set up in the lounge. The rest of the *Titanic* survivors had similar sleeping arrangements. Violet Jessop, of course, asked to be bunked with the children.

"We've stuck together this long," she told them. "I imagine staying together for the rest of the voyage is best for all of us."

Late on April 18, the *Carpathia* moved slowly toward New York Harbor. Voices rang out from outside the lounge.

Maya, Tucker, and Liam climbed off of their cots. Violet was already at the door. The four of them hurried up to the deck.

The railings were crowded with other survivors. Everyone was pointing and shouting. This time, it was in celebration.

On the horizon, a bright light glowed high in the sky. As the ship drew near, everyone onboard recognized the shape of a woman in robes, holding a torch high above her head to guide ships into America. It was the Statue of Liberty.

Maya and Tucker looked at each other and grinned. Violet seemed excited too. She put an arm around each of the children.

Tucker turned, looking for Liam. But when he found his friend standing behind them, Tucker's smile faded. Liam didn't look happy. He wasn't smiling. He dropped his head and looked at his feet.

Tucker realized that this must be completely different from how Liam had imagined his arrival

in America. Instead of arriving on *Titanic* with his parents, he was arriving as an orphan, alone.

The other survivors seemed to remember the same truth at the same time. Even the first-class passengers, some of whom had their families intact, had witnessed the tragedy when *Titanic* sank. The cheering subsided completely as the *Carpathia* moved along the south end of Manhattan Island. The ship steamed north, up the Hudson River.

Tucker and Maya had been to New York City before, but this was nothing like what they remembered. This skyline was much shorter, for one thing. Some of the most famous buildings, like the Empire State Building and the Chrysler Building, hadn't even been built yet.

"It's so different," Maya whispered. Tucker nodded. Still, New York City was an impressive sight, especially after so many days on the open ocean.

The *Carpathia* finally docked at Pier 54, on Manhattan's west side. The crowd that had gathered to greet the ship was impossibly large. It reminded Tucker and Maya of the crowd that had gathered to see *Titanic* off on her maiden voyage not that long ago.

"All of New York must be here," Violet said as she waved her handkerchief at the crowd gathered on the docks. "I don't suppose you see your aunt, Liam?"

Liam scanned the massive crowd. "Well, to be honest," he said, "from up here, it's impossible to pick out one single person down there."

"Well, I'm sure she's expecting you," Violet said reassuringly. "I'd guess she's near the front and close to the gangplank. She's probably anxious to find you."

"Maybe so," Liam said. "She could very well be that woman right there," he added, pointing at a figure at the front of the crowd. "The thing is, I wouldn't know."

Tucker slapped his forehead. "I totally forgot," he said. "Your father told us before we even left Ireland. You don't know her."

Liam nodded as his eyes filled with tears. "I've never even met her," he said quietly.

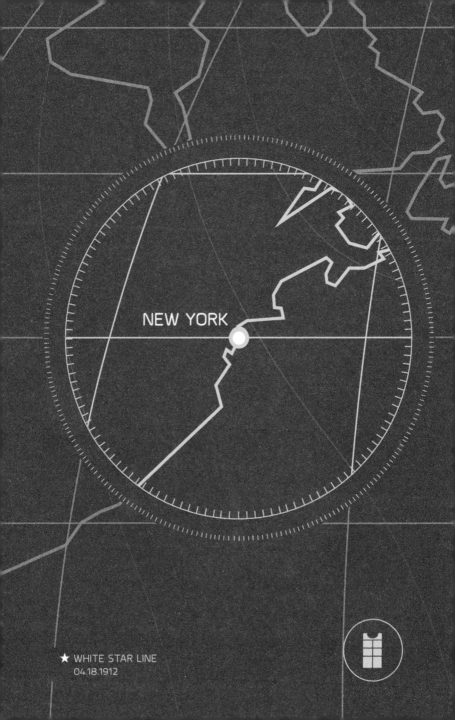

NEW YORK

★ WHITE STAR LINE
04.18.1912

11

PIER 54

The three children made their way down the gangplank with Violet close behind them. She kept her arms around them and urged them on like a mother goose leading her goslings.

Once they reached the docks, she ushered the children forward through the crowd. It seemed like most of the crowd was simply waving flags and throwing confetti as they cheered for the survivors of the *Titanic* and the heroic crew of the *Carpathia*.

Violet led the children to a small building just off the pier. A large group of *Titanic* passengers were gathered there. Maya noticed that many of them were children. She wondered if they all had aunts or uncles or cousins — anyone — waiting for them in New York.

"You three wait right here," Violet told the children. "I'll find someone in charge. We'll find your aunt, Liam. Don't you fret."

Liam, Maya, and Tucker stood there quietly while Violet spoke with two men. Based on their uniforms, Tucker guessed they were New York City police officers.

"Um, what about you two?" Liam finally asked.

"What about us?" Maya replied.

"Well, I know you've been saying you're from the future," Liam began.

"I thought you believed us," Tucker said.

Liam shrugged. "I don't know," he said. "And besides, even if it is true, you're here alone too, right? Your parents aren't here, in New York, in 1912. Right?"

"That's true," Maya said. "But —" She was about to explain that she and Tucker could get back whenever they wanted, that they'd already been back to 2012 several times since they first met Liam on the docks in Ireland. But at that moment, a woman approached them.

"Liam?" the woman said. She moved closer to the children, slowly. "Is that you, Liam?"

The woman was short and skinny, almost frail looking. Her hair was fiery red and pinned up on top of her head. Her clothes didn't appear to be much neater or cleaner than Liam's, and his had been through the *Titanic* sinking.

Liam looked up.

She smiled at him. "Liam Kearney," the woman said. "I know you don't know me. But I recognize you from the photo your mum sent last Christmas."

Liam moved closer to Maya and Tucker. He looked at his feet.

"I'm your aunt Moira," the woman said. "I'm your da's sister."

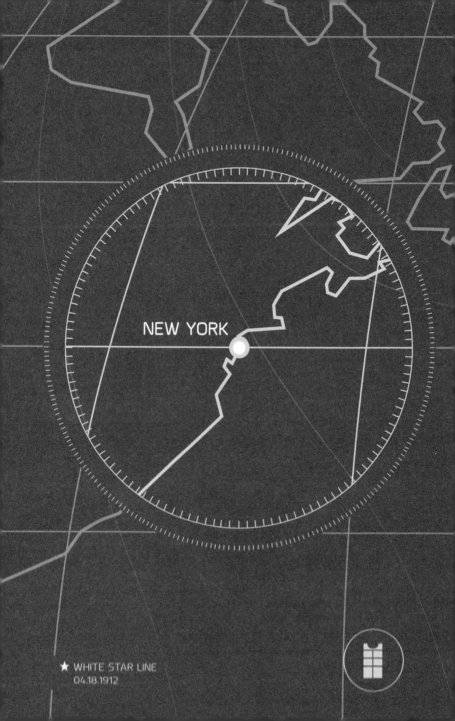

NEW YORK

12

AUNT MOIRA

Liam looked up at his aunt's face. "Hello," he said timidly. "It's nice to meet you."

Moira laughed. Then she threw her arms around her nephew. Tucker saw that she was crying as she laughed. It seemed odd to do both at once.

Maya sniffed loudly.

"You're not crying too, are you?" Tucker asked. "You aren't the crying type."

"Oh, zip it," Maya said. "I think Aunt Moira is going to make a great mom for Liam."

Suddenly Tucker had a sense of déjà vu as he watched the scene in front of him. Liam and

Moira hugging reminded him of something — a picture his mom kept on the mantel at home. It was a photo his dad had taken a few years ago of Tucker and his mom hugging. It looked just like what he was seeing now.

A chill ran up Tucker's spine, and he suddenly remembered what his mother had told him and Maya on their first day at the museum. It seemed like it had been ages ago, instead of just a few days.

"You should be especially interested in helping," his mother had told him when he'd argued about being there. "Your great-great-grandfather was a passenger onboard the *Titanic.*"

As Tucker stared at Liam he had a moment of clarity.

Liam isn't just some random Irish boy we met on the docks, he realized. He wasn't just a boy orphaned by the *Titanic*'s sinking. He and Tucker had a special connection. Tucker had felt it right away. That's why he'd been so concerned for Liam. It's why he'd kept insisting that he and Maya go back in time, again and again, to help him.

"Oh, man —" Tucker said. "I think Liam might be my great-great-grandfather."

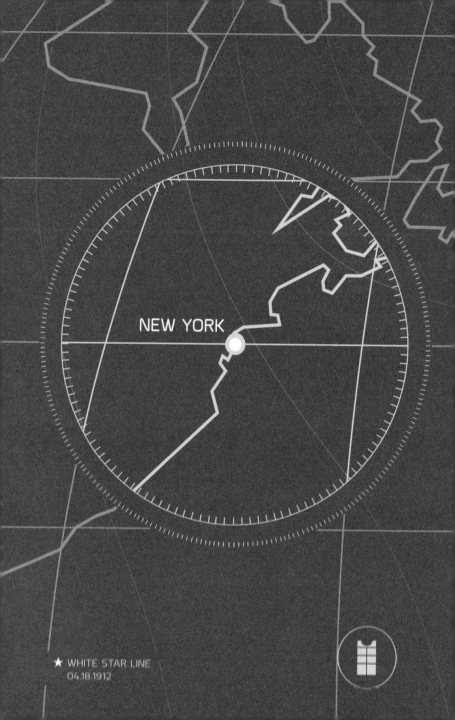

NEW YORK

DESTINY

13

"He's what?" Aunt Moira said.

"What did you just say?" Violet said.

Maya didn't say anything, but her mouth dropped open as she looked back and forth between the boys.

Liam's eyes widened in disbelief. Tucker grabbed his arm and pulled him aside.

Maya hurried over to Moira and Violet, cutting them off before they could follow the two boys. "Um, just ignore him," Maya said. "He's just really tired from, well, everything. Too much sea air . . . you know how it is. So, Moira. Tell me about you."

Tucker and Liam stood a few feet away.

"I know this is weird," Tucker said. "But the truth is, Maya and I are from the future." His face made it clear he wasn't kidding around.

Liam nodded once. Tucker could tell he firmly believed them now.

"And, well," Tucker went on, not sure how to continue. Finally he just blurted out the whole story. How his ancestor had survived the sinking, but had lost his parents and been raised by his aunt, a woman named Moira. He even explained about the ticket, the teacup, the violin, and finally the life vest.

When Tucker was done explaining, Liam was silent, taking it all in. Finally, he smiled. "You know," he said, "I have to admit, I felt there was a connection between you and me, right from the first time we met."

"I knew it too," Tucker said. "Like I was destined to meet you."

Maya wandered over and threw an arm

around each of their shoulders. "You two are having quite a moment, aren't you?" she joked.

Just then, a loud voice interrupted them. "You three!"

The three kids turned around. A short man in a round little hat stood there, grinning at them. He stood behind a big, old-fashioned camera balanced on a tripod. "Look this way," the man said.

There was a flash of light and a click.

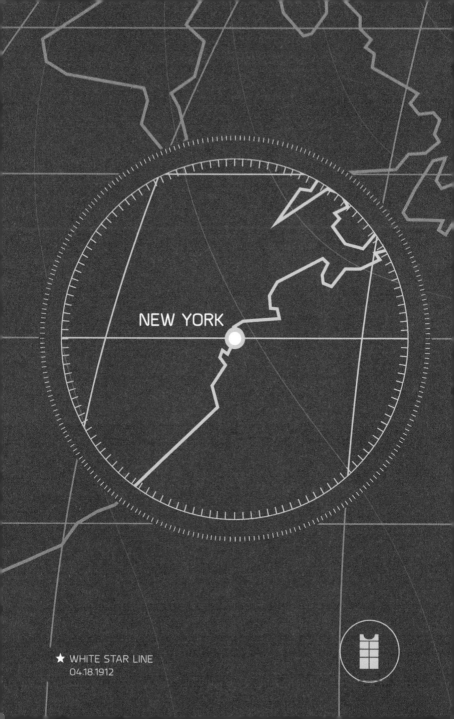

NEW YORK

★ WHITE STAR LINE
04.18.1912

14

SAYING GOODBYE

Minutes later, Tucker sighed. Aunt Moira had already given him and Maya big hugs and thanked them for helping her nephew on the *Titanic*. He could tell she was anxious to get Liam away from the crowds still gathered at the docks.

They probably need some time alone, Tucker thought. "Well, I guess it's time to say goodbye," he said.

"Are you sure you two don't need some help?" Violet asked Tucker and Maya. "I hate to think of two kids your age on your own in New York City, with no one here to meet you."

"We'll be fine," Maya assured her.

"Right," Tucker added. "We'll be home in no time."

Violet got down on her knees and threw her arms around them. "You two, be careful," she whispered, hugging them tightly. "And if you're ever in England, come by and visit me, will you?"

"Of course we will," Maya said. "I'm sure the museum has another box of Special Collection artifacts someplace. Right, Tucker?"

"Definitely," Tucker replied. "Let's see . . . early 1900s . . . I'm sure we have an exhibit on World War I. Maybe some of those items are magic too."

"World War . . . what?" Violet asked, sounding horrified.

"Nothing!" Maya said quickly. She clamped a hand over Tucker's mouth. "He was making a joke. A very bad joke." She glared at Tucker.

Luckily, Violet didn't ask any more questions. She just shook her head, seeming to accept that when it came to Tucker and Maya, there were some things she just wouldn't understand.

Violet leaned over and gave Liam a long hug as well. "You take care now, you hear?" she said. "You be a good boy for your aunt and make your mum and da proud."

Liam nodded. Tucker could see he was holding back tears at the mention of his parents. As Violet walked away, Liam moved over to stand in front of Maya and Tucker.

"I'm glad I ran into you two," Liam said. "Even

though when I first met you on the docks in Ireland, I thought you were the oddest children in the world."

"We're glad too," Maya said. "And we're sorry we held you up. You never did make it to the sweets shop that day, did you?"

Liam shook his head.

"Then I have a treat for you," Maya said. She reached into her messenger bag and pulled out three candies — the ones she'd grabbed from the bowl back at the museum. It seemed like a lifetime ago.

"Here you go," she said. She handed them to Liam.

"Thanks!" Liam said, unwrapping one and popping it into his mouth. He studied the wrapper in his hand. "I've never seen this kind before."

"Well, that sort of makes sense," Maya said. "I brought them with me from — well, you know."

Liam nodded. "Ah," he said. Then he winked. "I won't tell anyone."

Maya laughed. Then she threw her arms around the boy. "I'll miss you, Liam," she said.

"I don't know what to say," Tucker said when Liam turned to him. "I've never had to say goodbye to my great-great-grandfather before."

"Imagine how I feel," Liam said. "You're my descendant."

Tucker looked at his feet. "Weird," he said.

"But here's what's weirder," Liam went on. "If you hadn't come back with Maya and helped me — told me what was going to happen — I might not have gotten onto a lifeboat. I might have drowned with my parents."

Tucker swallowed hard. Liam was being so brave about losing his parents. If Tucker had lost his parents like that, he was sure he'd be a total mess.

"So in a way," Liam continued, "you coming back in time didn't just save me, but you, as well."

Tucker thought about it for a moment. All the connections made his head spin. He had to stop. It hurt his head too much.

Suddenly, Maya grabbed Tucker's arm. "Look," she said, pointing across the dock.

Tucker turned. A couple of police officers were talking with a member of the *Titanic* crew. The three men were watching Maya and Tucker closely.

"What do you think they're talking about?" Maya asked. She sounded a little nervous.

"I don't know," Tucker said. "But I think that man from the *Titanic* is one of the crewmembers who chased us all over the ship on our second trip when Mr. Kearney told people we were stowaways."

"Then we'd better get out of here," Maya said. "If they grab us and take away my bag, we'll be stuck here for good."

Tucker nodded. It was time to go back.

"Bye, Liam," Tucker said. He gave him a quick hug.

"Good luck," Liam said. "And thank you."

"Okay, let's do this," Maya said. She reached into her bag and pulled out the life vest . "Here, hold this," she told Tucker.

Tucker reached out and gripped the life vest tightly. Maya held firmly to the other half.

"On the count of three," Maya said. "One, two . . . three!"

Maya and Tucker pulled violently, and the life vest ripped in two.

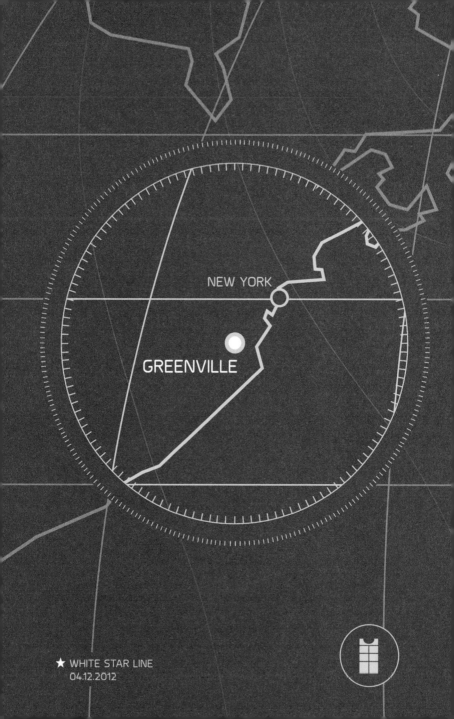

15

UNIDENTIFIED CHILDREN

Tucker sat up and opened his eyes. They were back in his bedroom in 2012. Maya's dad was still pounding on the door. Hardly any time had passed at all. It seemed unbelievable, especially considering how long they'd been in 1912.

"I hope that was the last time," Tucker said, groaning. "I don't know if my head can take any more time travel."

"We're out of Special Collection items," Maya pointed out. "So I can pretty much guarantee that was our last time."

Tucker sat up and put his head in his hands. "Oh, it hurts," he complained.

"Must be harder for boys," Maya said cheerfully. She was already on her feet. "I could time travel every day. I think it feels great."

"Maya!" her father shouted. He banged on Tucker's door three times. "I'm going to count to three, and then this door had better be open. One!"

Maya yanked off the borrowed parka she was still wearing. "Gotta go," she said. "I'll see you later, Tucker."

"Two!" boomed her father's voice.

"Bye," Tucker said. "And thanks."

Maya smiled at him.

"Three!" her father shouted.

Maya opened the door. "Hi, Dad," she chirped. She patted her bag. "I found my phone. Let's get going. You don't want to be late for work!"

Maya zipped past her dad and down the steps. Her father stood there for a moment, looking dumbfounded as he stared into Tucker's room.

Tucker looked at him and smiled. "Hey, Mr. Cho," Tucker said. "Nice morning, isn't it?"

Mr. Cho just stared at him for a minute. Then he shook his head and hurried down the steps after his daughter.

The babysitter stood in the open doorway, glaring at Tucker. "You're in big trouble," she said.

"Why?" Tucker asked. "I haven't even left this room. It's not my fault you let Maya come in."

"Let her come in?!" the babysitter echoed in disbelief.

Tucker nodded. "In fact," he said, "it kind of seems like you're the one who's in trouble. My mom is going to be pretty angry when she hears that you disobeyed her orders to keep Maya out of the house."

"I —" the babysitter started. But Tucker closed the door before she could finish.

Tucker flopped back on his bed. He was both happy and sad their *Titanic* adventure seemed to be over. But mostly he was relieved that he and Maya had helped Liam.

Then Tucker had an idea. He jumped up from his bed and turned on his computer. A quick Internet search brought up a huge list of photos and articles about the *Titanic*.

Tucker scrolled through the links and photos. Most were of the *Titanic* itself, still at the docks in Ireland or England. Some were photos of the *Titanic* still being built. Still others were paintings — artists' imaginings — of the *Titanic* sinking, or of the survivors being rescued.

He spent a long time looking at a photograph of a *Titanic* lifeboat pulling up alongside the *Carpathia*.

I wonder if I met any of the people on that boat, he thought.

Tucker kept searching. None of those were what he was looking for.

The last photo he found was a scan of a

newspaper clipping someone had saved from a hundred years ago. It was from a New York newspaper, and the headline read, "*Titanic* Tragedy Brings Great Loss and New Friends." Beneath the headline was a black-and-white photo. Tucker immediately recognized Liam standing to the right.

Standing with him were two other children. The caption identified Liam as "an Irish orphan and *Titanic* survivor." The other two kids were simply labeled, "Two unidentified American children whose guardians could not be found."

Tucker skimmed the article below the photo. The reporter had written, "The two American children vanished shortly after this photo was taken."

Tucker smiled to himself. Of course, he knew who they were immediately.

TITANIC TRAGEDY BRINGS GREAT LOSS AND NEW FRIENDS

Shown here: at right, an Irish orphan and *Titanic* survivor with two unidentified American children whose guardians could not be found.

RETURN TO
TITANIC

1 2 3 4

END

RETURN TO TITANIC

TIME VOYAGE

by STEVE BREZENOFF

1

RETURN TO TITANIC

STOWAWAYS

by STEVE BREZENOFF

2

RETURN TO TITANIC

AN UNSINKABLE SHIP

by STEVE BREZENOFF

3

RETURN TO TITANIC

OVERBOARD

by STEVE BREZENOFF

4

PASSENGER MANIFEST

While Tucker, Maya, and Liam are all fictional characters, the story of the *RMS Titanic* and its passengers is very real. In fact, some characters throughout the "Return to Titanic" series are based on real people.

1		**JOHN COFFEY** FIREMAN
2		**VIOLET JESSOP** STEWARDESS
3		**JOHN JACOB ASTOR IV** FIRST-CLASS PASSENGER
4		**EDWARD SMITH** CAPTAIN

Edward J. Smith

EDWARD SMITH

Captain Edward John Smith, a character featured in the "Return to Titanic" series, was the officer in command of the *Titanic* when it set off on its maiden voyage.

Captain Smith joined the White Star Line in 1880 and had been commanding ships for 25 years by the time *Titanic* set sail. On the night of the sinking, Captain Smith was awaked by the collision with the iceberg and rushed to the bridge. When told what had happened, Captain Smith ordered an inspection of the ship, which revealed that water had already risen 14 feet in the front of the ship. *Titanic* would only stay afloat for a few hours.

Little is known about Captain Smith's final hours aboard the *Titanic*. After giving the order to abandon ship, he was last seen on the ship's bridge. It is believed that Captain Smith went down with his ship. His body, if recovered, was never identified.

HISTORICAL FILES

1,500 people were thrown into the Atlantic Ocean when *Titanic* sank on April 15, 1912. Even though 18 lifeboats floated nearby, many survivors were afraid to go back for those in the water for fear the lifeboats would be swamped or pulled down by the suction from *Titanic* sinking. Only two lifeboats, lifeboat four and lifeboat fourteen, attempted to rescue people after the sinking. Lifeboat four rescued five people, two of whom later passed away. Lifeboat fourteen rescued four people, one of whom later died.

Titanic life vest circa 1912

After picking up *Titanic*'s distress call, the ocean liner *Carpathia* rushed to the last location given by *Titanic*'s radio operator. When the *Carpathia* arrived at 3:30 a.m., however, *Titanic* was gone. The crew of the *Carpathia* picked up the first lifeboat just after 4 a.m. By 8:30 a.m., the last lifeboat had been picked up, and *Carpathia* headed for New York.

On April 18, 1912, *Carpathia* docked at Pier 54 in New York. Aboard the ship were 711 survivors from *Titanic*. Less than one third of *Titanic*'s original passengers survived the sinking. The majority of passengers died from hypothermia as a result of the water temperature, which was a freezing 28 degrees the night of the sinking. In that temperature, death could occur in as few as 15 minutes.

The last living survivor from the *Titanic* was Millvina Dean, who was only nine weeks old when *Titanic* sank. She was the youngest passenger aboard the ship. Millvina Dean passed away on May 31, 2009.

Front page *Titanic* news story
The *San Francisco Call*
April 16, 1912

1300 PERISH IN WRECK OF THE TITANIC

Only 866 Saved When World's Greatest Liner Sinks at Sea

AUTHOR

Steve Brezenoff lives in St. Paul, Minnesota, with his wife, Beth, their son, Sam, and their small, smelly dog, Harry. Besides writing books, he enjoys playing video games, riding his bicycle, and helping middle-school students to improve their writing skills. Steve's ideas almost always come to him in his dreams, so he does his best writing in his pajamas.

ILLUSTRATOR

At a young age, Scott Murphy filled countless sketchbooks with video game and comic book characters. After being convinced by his high school art teacher that he could make a living creating what he loves, Scott jumped headfirst into the artistic pool and hasn't come up for air since. He currently resides in New York City and loves every minute of it.

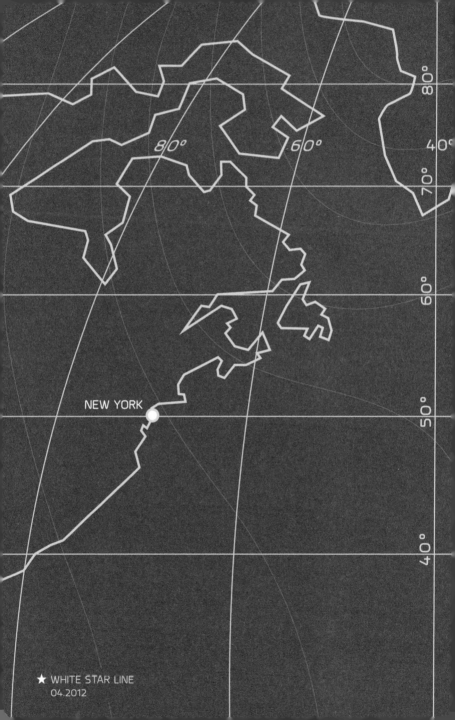

NEW YORK

★ WHITE STAR LINE
04.2012